D0645819

For Maria and Nicholas
— J.P.

For Shirley and Richard
— J.S.

Text copyright © 1994 by James Preller.
Illustrations copyright © 1994 by Jeffrey Scherer.
All rights reserved. Published by Scholastic Inc.
Printed in the U.S.A.
ISBN 0-590-48189-4

3 4 5 6 7 8 9 10   23   00 99 98 97 96 95

Wake Me in Spring

by James Preller
Illustrated by Jeffrey Scherer

SCHOLASTIC INC.
New York Toronto London Auckland Sydney

Mouse looked out
from his hole and said,
"It's getting cold."
He shivered.

Bear scratched his belly
and yawned.

"Yes," said Bear.
"I feel winter in my bones."

Bear looked at the calendar.
"Time for bed!" he said.
"I'm so tired.
I will surely sleep
all winter long."

"But Bear,"
Mouse cried,
"you'll miss
winter!"

Bear yawned and said,
"I'm so sleepy. I don't care."

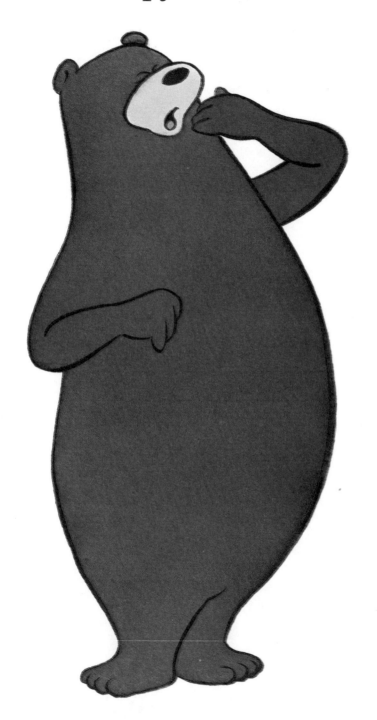

Mouse waved his arms.

"You will miss sleigh rides
in the snow!" said Mouse.

Bear rubbed his eyes and said,
"I'm so sleepy. I don't care."

"You will miss
hot chocolate
in steaming cups,"
said Mouse.

Bear pulled the curtains.
"I don't care," he said.

"You will miss ice skates on frozen lakes," said Mouse.

Bear locked the front door
and said, "I don't care."

"You will miss snowmen
with carrot noses!"
cried Mouse.

Bear only sighed and said, "I don't care."

Mouse didn't say a word.

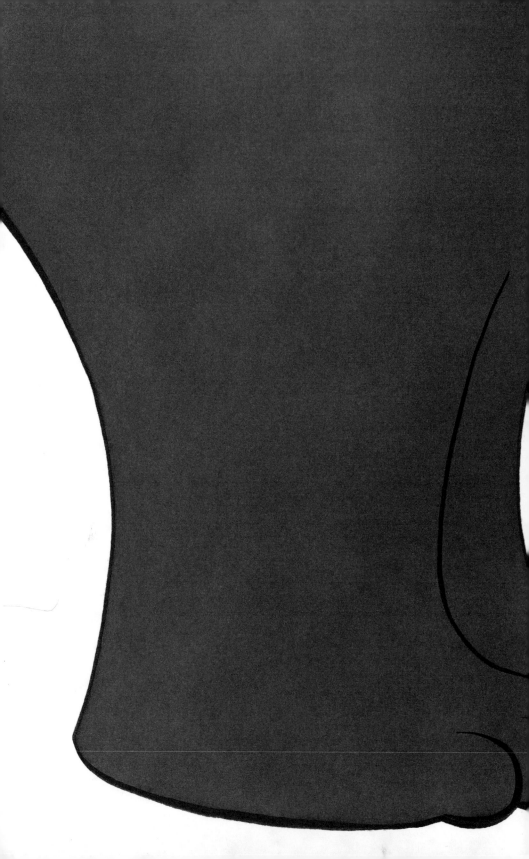

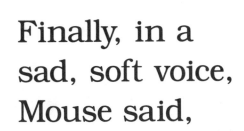

Finally, in a
sad, soft voice,
Mouse said,

"And I will
miss you."

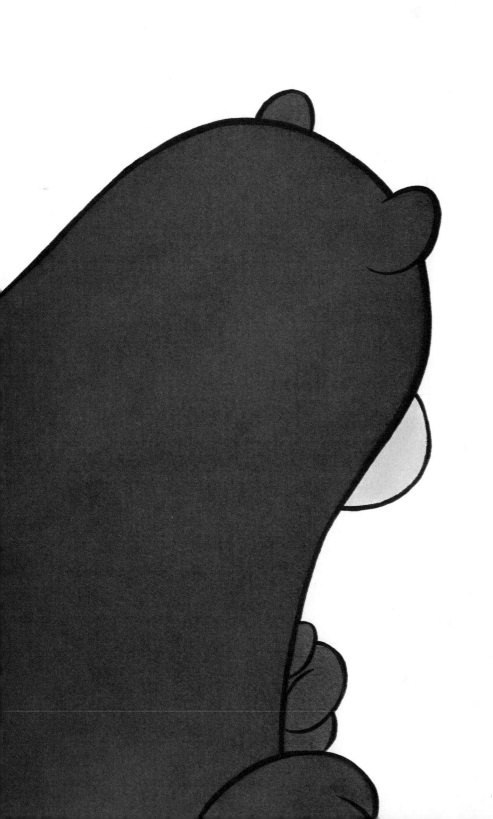

Bear
looked
into
Mouse's
watery
eyes.

Bear said, "Mouse,
I will not miss

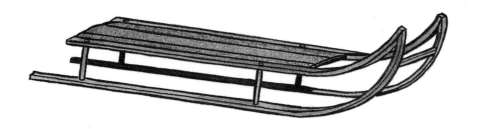

sleigh rides in the snow,

hot chocolate
in steaming
cups,

ice skates on frozen lakes,

or even snowmen
with carrot noses.

But I will
miss you.
I will miss you
very much."

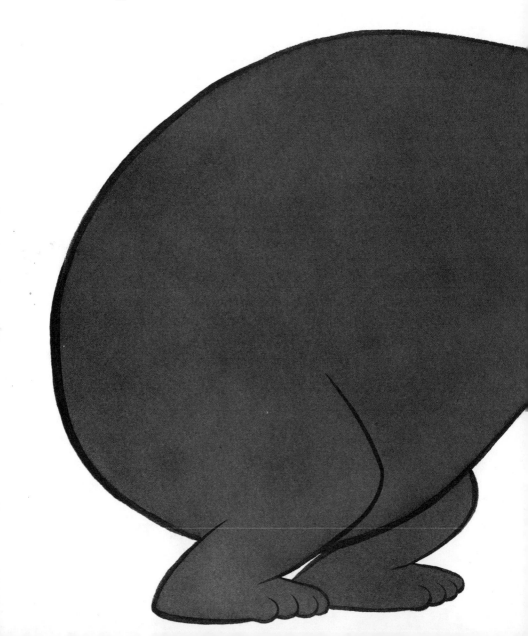

Bear bent down
and gave his friend
the kind of hug
that bears give best . . .

. . . a hug that
lasts all
winter.

"My little friend,"
Bear explained,
"please understand.
A bear needs to sleep
all winter long."

Mouse sniffed and
blew his nose. *Kerhonk!*

Bear brushed his teeth
and said, "Mouse,
I feel winter
in my bones.

Please wake me
in spring
when flowers bloom
and birds sing."

Mouse tucked Bear
into bed and whispered,
"Good night, Bear.
Sleep tight.

I'll see you in spring when flowers bloom . . .

. . . and best friends sing!"